THIS **ELEPHANT & PIGGIE** BOOK
BELONGS TO:

_____

_____

_____

For Oom Robbie

I Will Surprise My Friend!

By **Mo Willems**

WALKER BOOKS
AND SUBSIDIARIES
LONDON · BOSTON · SYDNEY · AUCKLAND

An **ELEPHANT & PIGGIE** Book

Hee hee hee!

4

Shhh… Here she comes!

11

14

Hee hee hee!

Hee hee hee!

24

31

34

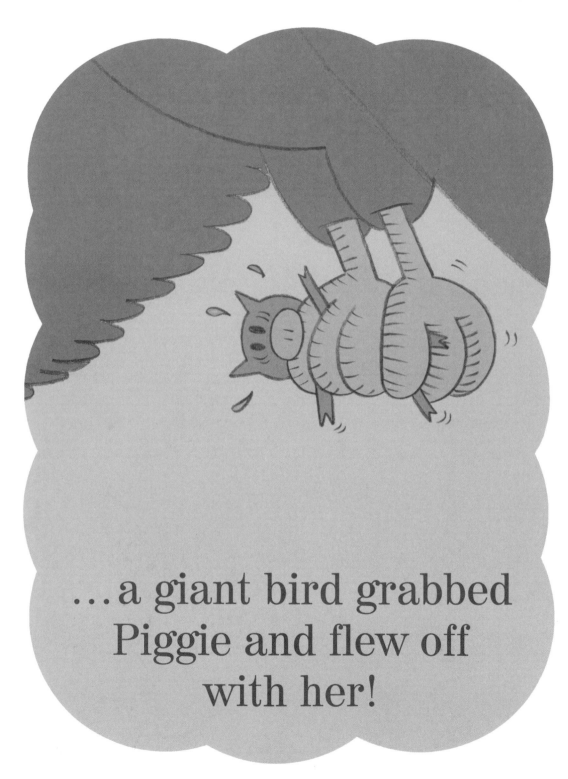

…a giant bird grabbed
Piggie and flew off
with her!

Or maybe...

...a scary, scary monster is trying to eat her right now!

44

46

That was a surprise.

A big surprise.

PLOP!

PLONK!

Mo Willems is the author of the Caldecott Honor-winning books
Knuffle Bunny: A Cautionary Tale and *Don't Let the Pigeon Drive the Bus!*
His other groundbreaking books include *Leonardo, the Terrible Monster*; *Edwina, the
Dinosaur Who Didn't Know She was Extinct* and *There Is a Bird on Your Head!*,
which won the American Library Association's 2008 Theodor Seuss Geisel Award
for the most distinguished book for beginner readers.

Mo began his career as a writer and animator on *Sesame Street*,
where he garnered six Emmy Awards.

This is a work of fiction. Names, characters, places and incidents are either
the product of the author's imagination or, if real, are used fictitiously.

First published in Great Britain 2008 by Walker Books Ltd
87 Vauxhall Walk, London SE11 5HJ

2 4 6 8 10 9 7 5 3 1

© 2008 Mo Willems

First published in the United States by Hyperion Books for Children.
British publication rights arranged with Sheldon Fogelman Agency, Inc.

The right of Mo Willems to be identified as author and illustrator of this work has been
asserted by him in accordance with the Copyright, Designs and Patents Act 1988

This book has been typeset in Century 725 and Grilled Cheese

Printed in Singapore

British Library Cataloguing in Publication Data:
a catalogue record for this book is available from the British Library

ISBN 978-1-4063-1472-4

www.walkerbooks.co.uk

www.pigeonpresents.com